AF585390
Winter
Spring

Blueberry Farm

Homegrown

A Scholastic Press book from Scholastic Australia

For: Happiness

Scholastic Press
An imprint of Scholastic Australia Pty Limited (ABN 11 000 614 577)
PO Box 579 Gosford NSW 2250
www.scholastic.com.au

Part of the Scholastic Group
Sydney • Auckland • New York • Toronto • London • Mexico City
New Delhi • Hong Kong • Buenos Aires • Puerto Rico

Published by Scholastic Australia in 2024.

Design by STINGart.

A catalogue record for this book is available from the National Library of Australia

ISBN: 978-1-76120-565-1

Typeset in Macarons and Drawzing.
Stephen Michael King created the illustrations using scribble and digital media.

Printed in China by RR Donnelley.
Scholastic Australia's policy, in association with RR Donnelley, is to use papers that are renewable and made efficiently from wood grown in responsibly managed forests, so as to minimise its environmental footprint.

10 9 8 7 6 5 4 3 2 1 24 25 26 27 28 / 2

Also available!

Thanks to Tiffany Malins, Margaret Connolly, Trish♥, Tanith and Luka.

smkbooks.com.au

Who will you meet today at

The warm season is when
we swim in the creek

and pick blueberries.

The windy season is when we
dance through the leaves,

and the cold season is when we all rug up.

Every season has days when
we wear our rain gear.

Shake
Shake.
Drip

Baa

There is a season that is
perfect for planting seeds.

Some seeds need to be
scattered on the breeze.

Some need to sit in rows
with a thin cover of soil.

Others like to go in deep
where they're safe and warm.

For many days and nights
Henna, Ziggs, Moe and
their farmyard friends
water . . .
watch . . .

and wait.

Then one morning,

the first new buds appear.

In a few weeks, they have grown big and strong.

Soon it's time for harvesting.

Comet the dog helps
to dig up the carrots.

Bubble Gum the pig
likes finding potatoes.

Clover the horse and Misty the donkey help
with the pumpkins and melons.

Blueberry Farm is filled with new, mouth-watering flavours . . .

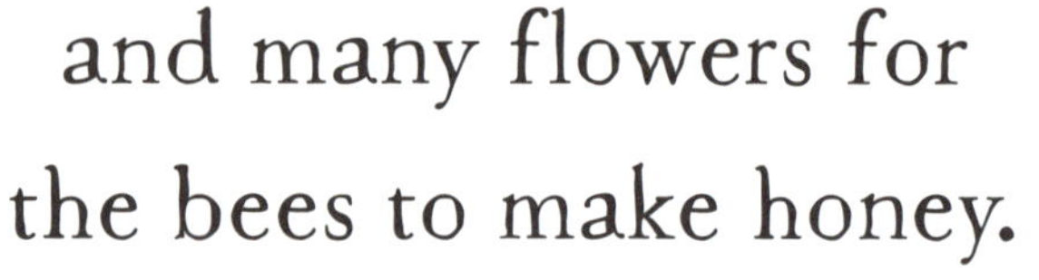

and many flowers for
the bees to make honey.

Henna, Ziggs and Moe love honey
for breakfast, lunch and dinner.

Blueberry Farm
Honey

Honey toast is Comet's favourite.

Summer
Autumn